DATE DUE			

C.2

E   Miller, M. L
Mil
        Those Bottles!

Bound to Stay Bound Books, Inc.

OCT 1 3 1994

THOSE BOTTLES!

by **M. L. Miller**

illustrated by **Barry Root**

G. P. Putnam's Sons • New York

Text copyright © 1994 by M. L. Miller. Illustrations copyright © 1994 by Barry Root
All rights reserved. This book, or parts thereof, may not be reproduced in any form without permission
in writing from the publisher.   G. P. Putnam's Sons, a division of The Putnam & Grosset Group,
200 Madison Avenue, New York, NY 10016.   G. P. Putnam's Sons, Reg. U.S. Pat. & Tm. Off.
Published simultaneously in Canada. Printed in Hong Kong by South China Printing Co. (1988) Ltd.
Book designed by Gunta Alexander. Text set in Vendome.
Library of Congress Cataloging-in-Publication Data
Miller, M. L. Those Bottles!/by M.L. Miller; illustrated by Barry Root.   p.   cm.
Summary: The Bottle family moves to the city to share their bottle-making talents, but they are not
accepted by their neighbors, until a disaster strikes. [1. Bottles—Fiction. 2. Prejudices—Fiction.]
I. Root, Barry L., ill. II. Title. PZ7.M627Th 1994 [E]—dc20 93-19684 CIP AC ISBN 0-399-22607-9
1 3 5 7 9 10 8 6 4 2
First Impression

To Arthur Levine—M.L.M.

For Nana Jo, with love—B.R.

Mr. Bottle drove his bottle through the Land of Bottles. His wife was a bottle. His children were bottles. His cat was a bottle and could not curl up.

One day they went to Mount Bottle and climbed to the cork. From there, through an incredible telescope, they looked northward for two hundred miles and saw a great city of lakes and waterfalls and monuments. But Mr. Bottle, who always said, "A land without bottles is no land at all," was shocked. For try as he might, in that city of people and crushable cans he could see not one single bottle.

So, then and there he became a bottle with a mission!
He pulled up stakes and took the entire family to that city
in the north to reveal the wonders of bottles to humans.

Once settled in their new home, the family got busy making new and better and better bottles in their work-shop. Bottles like birdbaths and blue mailbox bottles and some like "The Thinker" for parks and town squares. They made telephone bottles inside telephone-booth bottles and backpacks of bottles and motorboats too.

Now, although the Bottles were good neighbors, the people all said of them, "Those Bottles! Why can't they be like the rest of us? Why must they always go around acting like bottles?"

Many times Mrs. Bottle was snubbed at the market.
And the haughty cats of the district stared straight *through*
their cat.

Things were especially hard for the Bottle children. They were cheerful and friendly, but the other kids had trouble accepting glass classmates. Most days at school they had a hollow, left-out feeling, except at Halloween. But their times at home with the family in the workshop were truly exciting.

And Mr. Bottle went right on driving his bottle and believing in bottles and inventing new bottles.

One night there was a terrible flood. It wasn't raining hard in the city, but far upriver it had been raining for days. Without warning, a dam broke and water swept down the valley into shops and schoolrooms and houses, catching everybody asleep. Everybody except Mr. Bottle, who was up late working on a new creation.

In a flash he had those bottles whizzing everywhere,
lighting the darkness, alerting the people, and passing out
vast numbers of bottles! Big bottles, little bottles, bottles
like steamer trunks and rocking-horse bottles and one like
Gibraltar and lunch boxes and duck decoys and fire hydrants
and a mummy case and cash registers and radiators and
podiums and a davenport and various Thinkers in small,
medium, and large.

And the people all got busy filling up bottles with flood water. Then these bottles were rushed to the last spot of dry land in the city and set row upon row and piled layer upon layer.

Everyone worked desperately to save the city.

At last the flood began to go down. And as the waters dropped lower and lower, the layers of bottles grew taller and taller—till they made a great monument that reached to the sky and glittered in the moonlight.

The next day, when the danger had passed, everyone gathered at that monument. Bands played long into the night and fireworks went off and the Governor spoke and each of the Bottles was awarded a medal. And the people all cried, "Thank goodness for those Bottles! Hip, hip, hurrah!"

So then the Bottles were very proud.

And their cat was so happy, he finally curled up.